This is
Claire.

And this is **Fluffy**.

This is Claire when she's 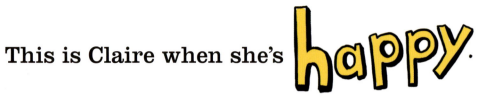 happy.

And this is Fluffy.

This is Claire when she's

sad.

And this is Fluffy.

This is Claire when she's **MAD!**

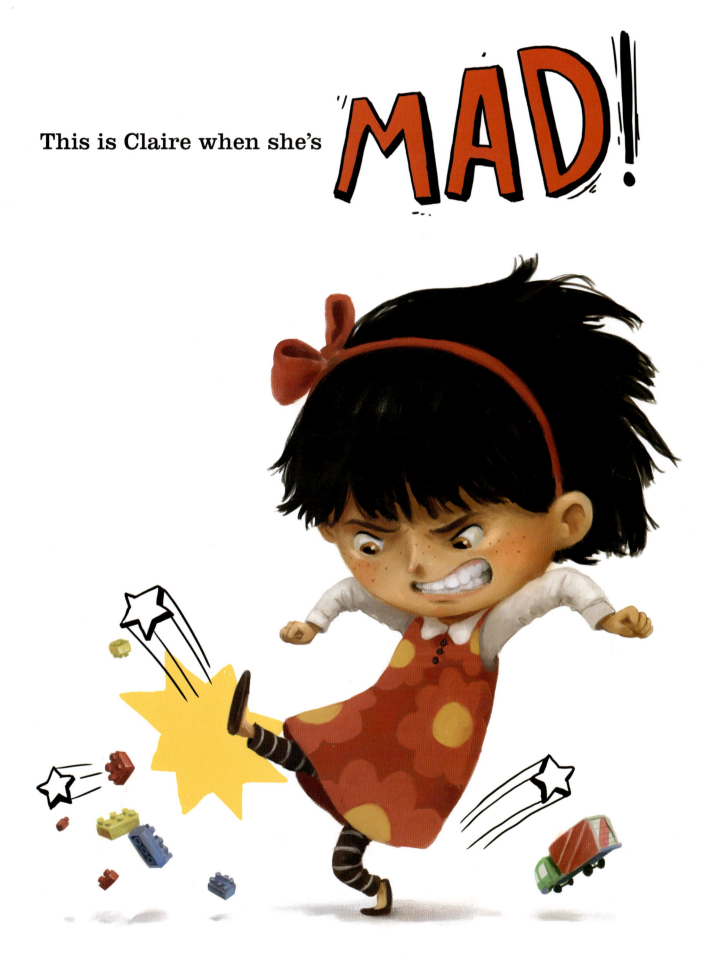

And let's just say we don't want to go there with Fluffy.

ATTACK OF THE 50-FOOT FLUFFY

by Mike Boldt

Margaret K. McElderry Books
New York London Toronto Sydney New Delhi

Claire is getting ready for the day. Fluffy has a matching outfit. How nice. Matching outfits make Claire happy. Fluffy looks happy too!

Those tiny buttons though, they're tricky.
You have to be careful or they'll . . .

Don't worry, Claire! It's not a problem.
We can fix it later.

It's time for breakfast anyway. Super Choco Puffs always make Claire very happy. Fluffy too! How could they not? They have super chocolatey marshmall . . .

UH-OH! Someone had the last bowl.

Don't worry, Claire. We're going shopping for groceries later! We'll add it to the list.

You know what makes Claire the happiest?
The Swing Set at the park.
Fluffy loves it too. There's nothing better
than swinging high in the air with the wind
in your face. I bet Claire and Fluffy could
spend all day on the swings.

WOW!

Looks like we weren't the only ones wanting to enjoy the weather. We've never seen a line like that for the swings before.

Well, we've got some time. Claire and Fluffy can just wait their turn. It probably won't take too long. . . .

Just a few more . . .

Any minute now.

Finally.

It's Claire and Fluffy's turn. Now they can swing to their heart's content.

Wait, what was that?

Don't worry, Claire, we can come back tomor—
Calm down, Claire, it's not worth getting upset over.
It's not the end of the world.

Okay.
Maybe that wasn't
the best choice of words.
Claire is mad (and so
is Fluffy).

RRRUNCH!

This wasn't supposed to happen.

This is Claire apologizing for wrecking everything.

Fluffy is also sorry.

"Don't worry, Claire. We forgive you. And Fluffy too. We've *all* been there before."

Claire and Fluffy are happy again, but tired, too!
Cleaning up all that mess was a lot of work.
Do you know what we think would be good now?

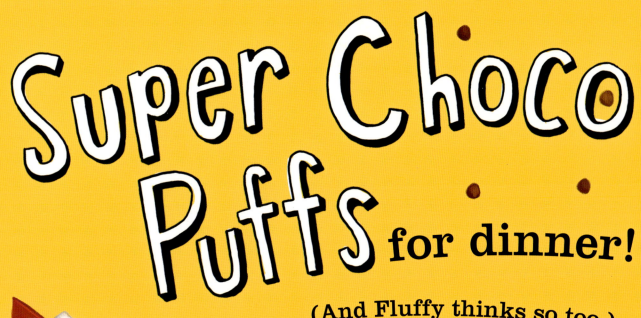

Super Choco Puffs for dinner!

(And Fluffy thinks so too.)

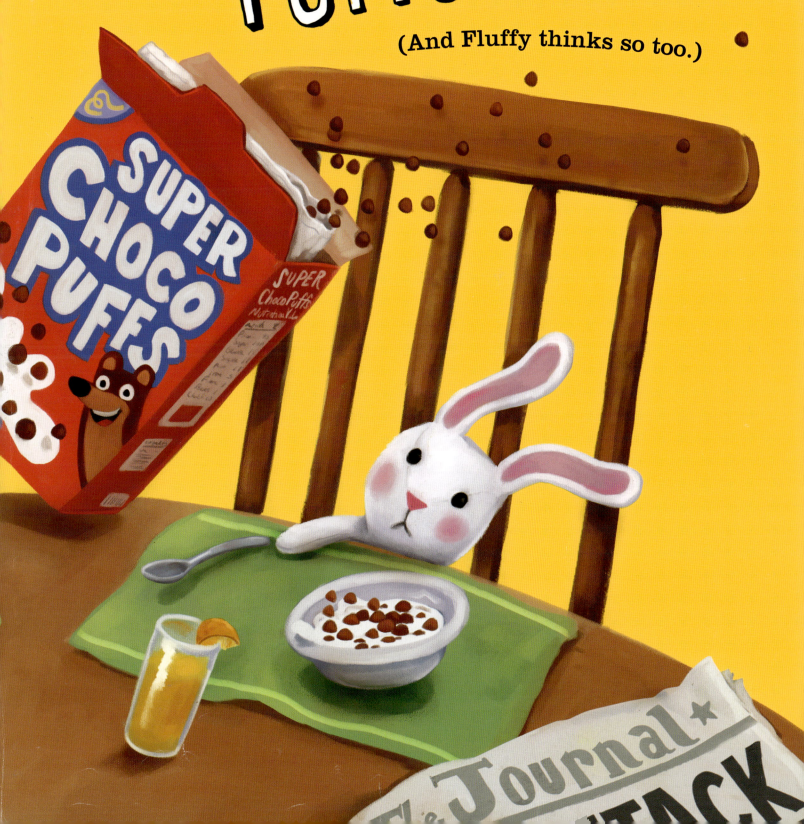

For Claire

MARGARET K. McELDERRY BOOKS

An imprint of Simon & Schuster Children's Publishing Division
1230 Avenue of the Americas, New York, New York 10020
Copyright © 2018 by Mike Boldt
All rights reserved, including the right of reproduction in whole or in part in any form.
MARGARET K. McELDERRY BOOKS is a trademark of Simon & Schuster, Inc.
For information about special discounts for bulk purchases, please contact Simon & Schuster Special Sales at
1-866-506-1949 or business@simonandschuster.com.
The Simon & Schuster Speakers Bureau can bring authors to your live event. For more information or to book an event,
contact the Simon & Schuster Speakers Bureau at 1-866-248-3049 or visit our website at www.simonspeakers.com.
Book design by Lauren Rille • The text for this book was set in Clarendon LT Std.
The illustrations for this book were rendered digitally.
Manufactured in China • 0518 SCP • First Edition
2 4 6 8 10 9 7 5 3 1
Library of Congress Cataloging-in-Publication Data
Names: Boldt, Mike, author, illustrator.
Title: Attack of the 50-foot Fluffy / Mike Boldt.
Other titles: Attack of the fifty-foot Fluffy
Description: First edition. | New York : Margaret K. McElderry Books, [2018] | Summary: Claire and her stuffed rabbit,
Fluffy, wake up happy but one thing goes wrong after another until, finally, Claire and Fluffy are both very, very angry.
Identifiers: LCCN 2017029903 | ISBN 9781481448871 (hardcover) | ISBN 9781481448888 (eBook)
Subjects: | CYAC: Temper tantrums—Fiction. | Behavior—Fiction. | Toys—Fiction.
Classification: LCC PZ7.B635863 Att 2018 (print) | DDC [E]—dc23
LC record available at https://lccn.loc.gov/2017029903